WILLIAMSBURG

CRADLE OF THE REVOLUTION

BOOKS BY RON AND NANCY GOOR

Heads

Insect Metamorphosis

Williamsburg: Cradle of the Revolution

WILLIAMSBURG

CRADLE *of the* REVOLUTION

RON and NANCY GOOR

Atheneum 1994 New York
Maxwell Macmillan Canada
Toronto
Maxwell Macmillan International
New York Oxford Singapore Sydney

The authors wish to thank the following people for
their help in the development of this book:
Catherine H. Grosfils, Susan Berg,
Elizabeth M. Hartjens, Edith Poindexter,
Alex Goor, and Dan Goor.

The photographs on pages 50 and 69 courtesy of the Colonial Williamsburg
Foundation; on pages 57, 75, and 78 courtesy of the Library of Congress; on
page 54 courtesy of Red Hill, The Patrick Henry National Monument,
Brookneal, Virginia.

Atheneum
Macmillan Publishing Company
866 Third Avenue
New York, NY 10022

Maxwell Macmillan Canada, Inc.
1200 Eglinton Avenue East
Suite 200
Don Mills, Ontario M3C 3N1

Macmillan Publishing Company is part of the Maxwell Communication
Group of Companies.

First edition

Printed in the United States of America

10   9   8   7   6   5   4   3   2   1

Design by Jaye Zinet
The text of this book is set in New Baskerville.

Library of Congress Cataloging-in-Publication Data
Goor, Ron.
Williamsburg : cradle of the revolution / by Ron and Nancy Goor. —
1st ed.
p.   cm.
Includes bibliographical references and index.
ISBN 0-689-31795-6
1. Williamsburg (Va.)—Social life and customs—Juvenile literature.
2. Virginia—Politics and government—1775–1783—Juvenile literature.
[1. Williamsburg (Va.)—Social life and customs.   2. Virginia—Politics
and government—1775–1783.]   I. Goor, Nancy.   II. Title.
F234.W7G65   1994
975.5'4252—dc20
94-9370

For the Colonial Williamsburg Foundation,
for helping make Williamsburg come alive, and for Marcia Marshall,
for helping make this book come alive

PREFACE

Today Williamsburg is a bustling city filled with tourists as well as actors playing their roles as eighteenth-century colonists. The town has been recreated to give visitors a feeling of what it was like to live in Williamsburg in colonial times. You can step into the silversmith's shop and watch him fashion a spoon from a flat piece of silver. You can eat Sally Lunn Muffins or Beef Steak and Ham Pye at one of the many colonial inns. You can sit on a hard bench in the House of Burgesses and know that Patrick Henry sat in that very spot and made a fiery speech that determined the destiny of our country.

The photographs in this book were taken in the restored colonial Williamsburg. The people pictured are actors dressed to look the way people looked who lived in Williamsburg during colonial times. Don't let these photographs confuse you. At 5:00 P.M., when Williamsburg closes, the "colonists" will change into their everyday clothes, drive home in their automobiles, cook dinner in their microwaves, and turn on their television sets.

But, try to forget they are just actors. Try to imagine that you are a colonist visiting Williamsburg—the most important center of revolutionary thinking during one of the most exciting times in history.

Along these peaceful streets walked some of the greatest men America has ever known: George Washington, Thomas Jefferson, Patrick Henry, George Mason, Richard Bland, George Wythe, and many more. These are the men who shaped the history of the United States. This is where they met— Williamsburg. This is where they developed and discussed the ideas and ideals that formed the basis of our Constitution and Declaration of Independence.

We call these men great Americans, yet they grew up loyal Englishmen. They weren't raised as rebels. In fact, they loved England dearly and wanted to remain loyal subjects. What events forced them to turn against their mother country? What did England do to cause the tremendous break? What series of events pushed a once loyal colonist to cry, "Give me liberty or give me death!"?

To answer these questions, we will explore Williamsburg in the 1760s and 1770s. In the eighteenth century, Williamsburg was the focal point of revolutionary thought. It attracted a group of thinkers and leaders of unparalleled talent.

Many of our founding fathers sharpened their political skills at the capitol in Williamsburg.

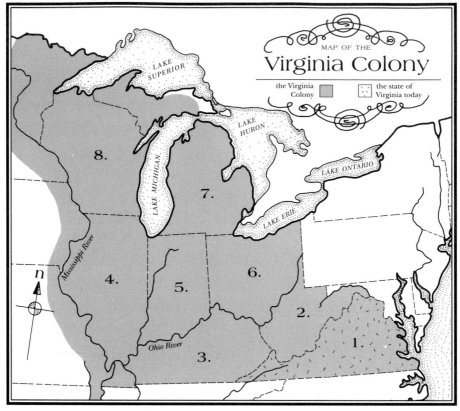

The Virginia Colony stretched over the land which is now occupied by the states of 1-Virginia; 2-West Virginia; 3-Kentucky; 4-Illinois; 5-Indiana; 6-Ohio; 7-Michigan; 8-Wisconsin.

MORE THAN JUST A COLONIAL TOWN

In colonial times, Williamsburg was a very important town. It was the seat of the government for the entire Virginia Colony from 1699, when the capital moved from Jamestown, to 1780, when the capital moved to Richmond. Virginia was the oldest and largest of all the English colonies. It had twice as many people as any other colony. The area was tremendous. It stretched from the East Coast all the way to the Mississippi River in the West and the Great Lakes in the North.

Williamsburg was the social, economic, and educational center for the whole colony. People came here from all corners of Virginia to do business at the capital. Young men came here to study at the College of William and Mary, which was one of the few institutions of higher learning in the colonies. It was in Williamsburg that the royal governor, appointed by the king of England, lived in the splendid Governor's Palace. In Williamsburg, the General Assembly met in the capitol to make laws for the colony. It was made up of the Council and the House of Burgesses, the first elected representatives in the New World. The court here tried the colony's most serious cases.

Williamsburg could boast of the first public mental hospital and the first theater in colonial America.

Because Williamsburg was such an important town, Francis Nicholson, the second colonial governor of Virginia, planned the city with great care. Influenced by Roman ideas, he designed the city like a Roman military camp, crossed by two main streets, the *decamus* and the *cardo*. The *decamus* was Duke of Gloucester Street. Ninety-nine feet wide and a mile long, it stretched between the capitol and the College of William and Mary. The *cardo* was England Street, which no longer exists.

In the early eighteenth century, the General Assembly set aside a large grassy area to be used for markets and fairs. From the early hours of the morning until late in the evening, Market Square was filled with noise and activity. Townspeople and their slaves came here to buy livestock and produce raised by local farmers. The sounds of lambs bleating, pigs squealing, and cows mooing mixed with the cries of farmers hawking their produce, slave dealers auctioning off slaves, and hucksters promoting plots of land or other goods.

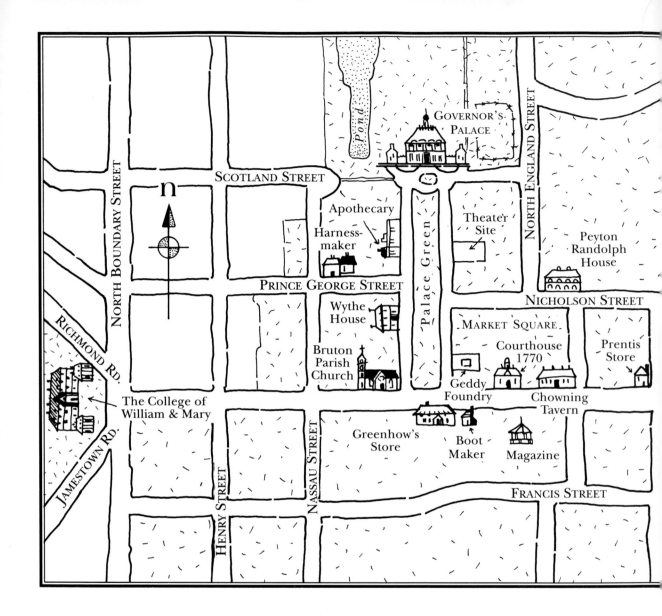

If you look at the map, you can find the most important landmarks. The capitol and the College of William and Mary are located at either end of Duke of Gloucester Street. Look for the Palace Green, which stretches to the north off of Duke of

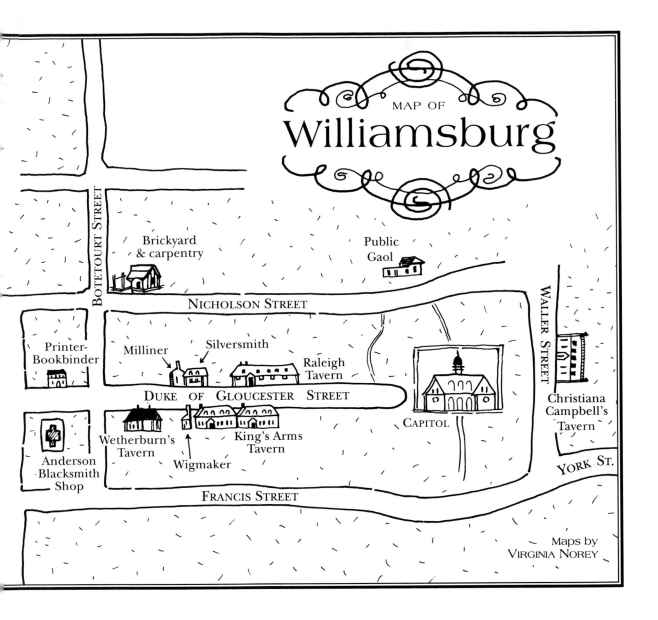

MAP OF
Williamsburg

BOTETOURT STREET

Brickyard & carpentry

Public Gaol

NICHOLSON STREET

WALLER STREET

Printer-Bookbinder

Milliner

Silversmith

Raleigh Tavern

Christiana Campbell's Tavern

DUKE OF GLOUCESTER STREET

CAPITOL

Anderson Blacksmith Shop

Wetherburn's Tavern

Wigmaker

King's Arms Tavern

YORK ST.

FRANCIS STREET

Maps by VIRGINIA NOREY

Gloucester Street. You will find the Governor's Palace at its tip. You can locate Bruton Church at its left. Market Square is the large grassy area behind the courthouse just east of the Palace Green.

7

The Williamsburg you see pictured in this book does not look exactly like Williamsburg did in 1765. There were no trees along Duke of Gloucester Street in colonial times. Besides being a fire hazard, trees along main boulevards were not fashionable. The roads were not paved. They were dusty and dirty when the weather was dry, and when it rained or snowed they turned into a sea of mud. Of course there were no streetlights. Electricity had not yet been discovered.

In colonial times, as today, colorful signs hung above the shop doors that line Duke of Gloucester Street. Because many people could not read, the shop signs illustrated the type of shop or the owner's name in pictures.

If you couldn't read, these signs would help you shop. Top left: Peter Hay's Shop (Hay was a pharmacist); top right: John Greenhow Store (sign shows Greenhow sells imported goods); bottom left: Josiah Chowning's Tavern; bottom right: bootmaker's shop.

TAVERNS AND INNS

The Raleigh Tavern, the King's Arms Tavern, and Wetherburn's Tavern were three of the many inns and taverns (often called ordinaries in colonial times) established to feed, entertain, and board the many people who came to Williamsburg during Publick Times, when the government was in session.

LIFE AT THE TAVERNS

The Williamsburg taverns were social gathering places. They provided food, drink, and lively conversation. The Raleigh Tavern was one of the finest taverns in Williamsburg. For the eighteenth century, it was luxurious. No more than *two* men were allowed to sleep together in a bed. (They rarely knew each other.) The Raleigh Tavern had thirty-six beds but could sleep seventy-five. Three slept on the floor. A gentleman paid seven and a half pence for a night's lodging. For an additional seven and a half pence, he could board his horse.

Like the Raleigh Tavern, Wetherburn's Tavern had a large dining room where a meal could be bought for a shilling. A meal might consist of a hearty stew, bread, and ale. At least two diners shared a trencher (wooden plate). Both ate with fingers or a spoon. Forks were not yet in use in England or the colonies. A tankard of beer was passed around the table and everyone took a swig.

Once a week in the evening, Mr. Wetherburn pushed back the tables and chairs in the large dining room and held a dance. It cost five shillings to join in the minuets, reels, quadrilles, and even a jig or two, plus ten shillings a quart for Mr. Wetherburn's famous punch. This was expensive entertainment considering craftsmen earned ten to twelve shillings a week. At the end of the evening, a guest would climb the stairs to his room and crawl into bed, careful not to disturb the stranger sleeping beside him.

Next morning, Wetherburn's rooster's loud cock-a-doodle-doo served as an alarm clock. A guest would dress without bathing (bathing was considered unhealthy, as it removed natural oils) or changing his clothes (the same clothes

When shaving, a colonist placed a bowl under his chin.

were worn for several days, a week, or more). Instead, a guest would dip into the porcelain bowl perched on his night table to splash some water on his face.

In the 1760s and 1770s, when the royal governor dissolved the House of Burgesses for defying Parliament or the Crown, the burgesses met in the Apollo Room of the Raleigh Tavern. Revolutionary leaders such as Thomas Jefferson, Patrick Henry, and George Wythe were often found here engaged in lively political or philosophical discussions.

An illustrated alphabet for children. J and U were not part of the colonial alphabet.

GENERAL STORES

Stores such as John Greenhow's were stocked with a multitude of imported goods. You could buy your quills, ink powder and notebooks, Irish linens, fashionable buttons, smoothing irons, ready-made shirts, elegant snuffboxes, fine prints by Hogarth, iron kettles, sponges, brooms, and tools for almost every occasion.

At Greenhow's you could purchase anything you might need or just enjoyed having. However, you had to use *ready* money (Spanish or Dutch coins). Mr. Greenhow accepted no credit. A popular form of money in the Virginia Colony was notes of credit made with London tobacco merchants and other kinds of promises to pay. Virginia colonists were forced to use these types of currency because England would not allow them to mint their own coins or to use English ones. Often they resorted to barter. A housewife might pay for a bag of sugar with a dozen eggs. When they could, townspeople bought on credit and took years to pay.

For a very special occasion, colonial parents might buy their child a toy cannon, a pinwheel, a stuffed sheep to pull, a toy drum, or a doll at Greenhow's Store.

When not protecting m'lady from the rain or snow, the calash bonnet *(back row, left) collapsed like a carriage top and could be stored flat. The* mobcap *(front row, left) was first worn by the lower classes. The* pinner *(front row, right) was worn under a larger hat. Women might wear a* lace cap *(back row, center) in the evening at home. When men removed their wigs at night they often wore an embroidered* nightcap *(back row, right) to cover their bald heads.*

MILLINER

For the fashion-conscious, clothes in the latest European style could either be ordered from abroad or made to order at a mantua (dressmaker) or milliner's shop such as Margaret Hunter's. (The word "milliner" comes from "Milaner"—a person who imported clothes from Milan, Italy, always a center of fashion.)

Miss Hunter also made hats for women. Upper-class women always wore hats to protect their faces from the sun. How mortifying if it were thought that a "lady" was suntanned from working in the fields.

Left: "Fashion babies" dressed in the latest styles were displayed in the milliner's shop to show colonial women what was fashionable in London or Europe.

Above right: Padded pudding caps were worn by toddlers to prevent their brains from turning to pudding when they fell on their heads.

Below right: The streets of Williamsburg were not paved in colonial times. Duke of Gloucester Street was so muddy it was described as being a mile long and a foot deep. At the milliner's, women could purchase clogs such as these to raise their cloth shoes above the mud and keep them relatively clean.

BARBER AND PERUKE MAKER

The Barber and Peruke (Wig) Maker was a popular shop in Williamsburg because Williamsburg was a center of power, and during colonial times, rich, powerful, and important people wore "big wigs." We use the expression "bigwig" today to describe the type of people who would have worn big wigs in colonial times.

In Williamsburg, men of all ages wore wigs—starting as early as age seven. Wigs were expensive (they could cost as much as a craftsman's earnings for a month) and they were uncomfortable. They squeezed the head and were hot and heavy. Most people took their wigs off when at home and covered their bald heads with little caps. Women in Williamsburg wore curls, rather than wigs. The social season was so short that it was not worth buying an expensive wig for a few dinners or balls during Publick Times.

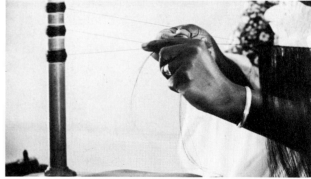

The wigmaker weaves (actually knots) a few strands of the prepared hair onto three silk threads. She slides the strands along the silk threads and pushes them tightly together to make a strip of hairs. Layer by layer she sews these strips of hair from the bottom to the top of a caul (fitted skull cap) and creates a wig.

Wigs came in different colors. White was for formal, social, or military occasions. For normal daily use, black, brown, gray, or grizzle (a mixture of black and white hair) was preferred. Wigs varied in price. Wigs made of human hair were most expensive. Cheaper wigs were made of horsehair, goat hair, calves' tails, silk, linen, or cotton thread.

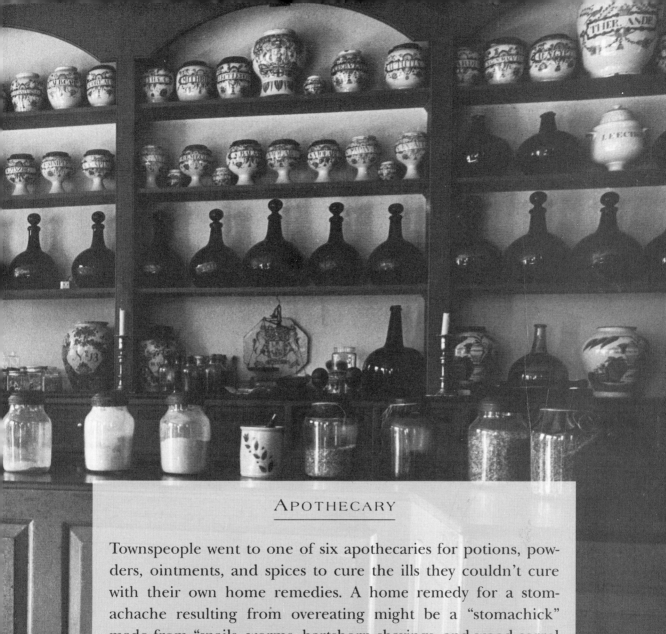

APOTHECARY

Townspeople went to one of six apothecaries for potions, powders, ointments, and spices to cure the ills they couldn't cure with their own home remedies. A home remedy for a stomachache resulting from overeating might be a "stomachick" made from "snails, worms, hartshorn shavings, and wood sorrel stewed in brandy and seasoned with spices and herbs." The apothecary sold Peruvian bark to reduce fevers, ipecac (Brazil root) to control vomiting, licorice and rock candy to soothe sore throats and calm coughing, calamus (sweet flag) to settle stomachs, and fennel to ease gas or colic.

The only known cure for a toothache was removal of the tooth. The military surgeon removed the soldier's tooth with a special key designed for the job. As anesthetics were not yet in use, when the surgeon pulled a tooth, sawed through a bone, or cut through the flesh to amputate a leg or arm, the patient drank as much rum as he could to deaden the pain.

The apothecary often had a medical degree from Europe. He performed amputations, bled customers to reduce their ill humors, and applied leeches to remove bruises.

SILVERSMITH

People shopped at the Williamsburg silversmiths to buy small silver pieces like spoons, cups, and shoe buckles crafted by the silversmiths, or to have their watches and clocks repaired. The large, ornate silver pieces that graced the tables and chests of the aristocratic Virginians were imported from London. Silver objects were enjoyed not only for their beauty; they were a wise investment. Colonists had no banks in which to store money safely. Instead, they converted their silver coins into silver serving pieces. Because they were in constant use, these serving pieces could not easily be stolen. And, unlike silver coins, silver objects were easily identified if they were taken. Even middle-class colonists owned some silver.

A silversmith files a silver wire at a workbench that accommodates five people. The floor is latticed to catch silver filings. Silver was not to be wasted. Periodically the filings were collected, melted down, and reused. The water-filled sphere at the worker's left is called a bocal. *In colonial times (before the electric bulb was invented), the bocal was used to focus light from a candle onto the silversmith's work area so he could see when the light was dim.*

Except for the colorful signs advertising their wares or function, stores and taverns in Williamsburg looked no different than private homes. In fact, most of the houses served as both shops and homes. The milliner, Margaret Hunter, lived in the attic above her store. James Anderson, the blacksmith, built seven forges behind his house to heat the fires that kept him and his blacksmiths busy making and repairing tools and, during the revolutionary war, weapons. The house that displayed the sign The Golden Ball was both shop and home to jeweler and goldsmith James Craig, his family of five, and his one slave.

In the neighborhoods off the main streets, you could find modest one-story bungalows one room deep as well as elegant many-roomed mansions. Many of the Williamsburg gentry lived in splendor and comfort. George Wythe, the lawyer, judge, burgess, and professor, who was Thomas Jefferson's mentor and teacher, inhabited a spacious estate on Palace Street. His stately brick home was equipped with the following outbuildings (buildings not attached to the house): kitchen, smokehouse, laundry, lumber house, fowl house, dovecote, stable, and two necessaries (outhouses).

Slaves often lived in cabins set apart from the main houses. The one large room two or three families occupied generally had a dirt floor and glassless windows with wooden coverings to keep out the cold.

NORMAL TIMES

For most of the year, Williamsburg was a quiet little country town. Many of the one thousand to two thousand residents (more than half were slaves) had jobs that helped keep the wheels of government turning. In addition, there were the professors, administrators, and students who filled the classrooms and offices at the College of William and Mary.

THE COLLEGE OF WILLIAM AND MARY

Originally planned in 1617 in order "that the Youth may be piously educated in good Letters and Manners, and the Christian Faith may be propagated amongst the Western Indians, to the Glory of Almighty God," the College of William and Mary was finally built in 1695. The second institution of higher learning in the colonies, it prepared men for teaching, the church, and public service. No longer would a Virginia boy have to go to England for an education. (Girls were rarely educated except at home.)

Because it was a center of education and thus of ideas, the College of William and Mary influenced and was influenced by the great leaders of the day. Thomas Jefferson, James Monroe, and John Marshall (chief justice of the Supreme Court from 1801 to 1835) were all educated here.

A classroom in the College of William and Mary

In the midst of leather, shoe forms, thread, tools, and half-finished shoes, the shoemaker punches holes into a sole he has just completed so he can stitch it to the "uppers" he has cut, and make a shoe.

Craftsmen, tailors, seamstresses, cooks, bakers, blacksmiths, wheelwrights, bricklayers, carpenters, cabinetmakers, music teachers, doctors, surgeons, lawyers, tavern keepers, grocers, saddlemakers, and merchants also contributed to the commercial life of Williamsburg.

Except for the milliners and several prominent innkeepers, the few women who had professional careers were widows who had taken over their husband's shops and professions. Clementina Rind, for example, became the editor of the *Virginia Gazette* in 1773, when her husband, William, died. Some women assisted their husbands in managing the shops often located in their homes.

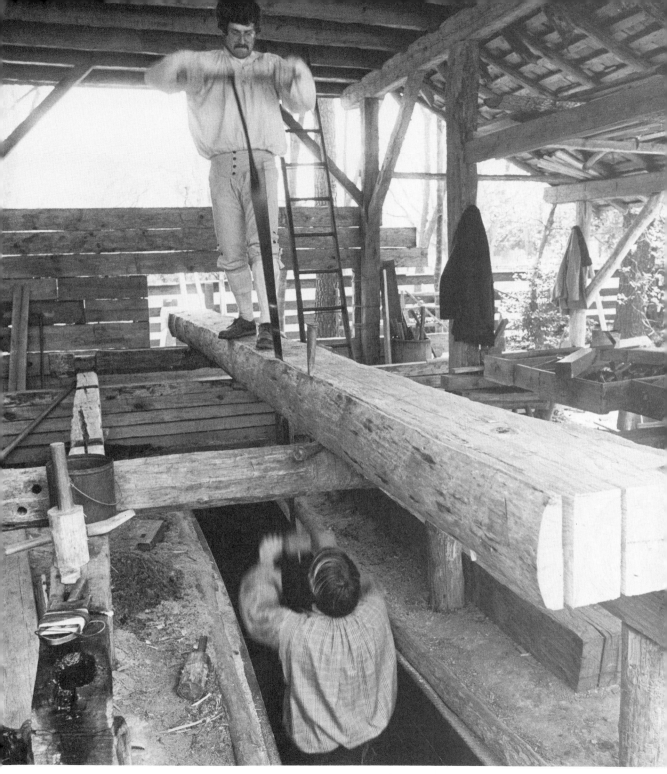

Housewrights (carpenters who framed and built houses) devised this special way to saw large logs into wooden boards.

For entertainment, colonial children rolled hoops, flew kites, and played marbles, hopscotch, leapfrog, and blindman's bluff. Their toys were few and many were made at home.

But most upper-class and middle-class Williamsburg women spent their days overseeing their households, their help (slaves and servants), and their multitudes of children.* They supervised their slaves and servants in tending the garden, raising chickens and rabbits, curing meats, pickling and preserving vegetables, and purchasing food at the local markets. They directed the preparation and serving of generous meals to their family and frequent guests. They hired tutors, music teachers, and dancing instructors to socialize their children. They organized schools to teach their sons reading, writing, arithmetic, and the classics and to teach their daughters reading, writing, arithmetic, and needlepoint. They entertained their many guests. Housewifery was a full-time job.

*Colonial men and women felt it a religious duty as well as a material investment to be fruitful and multiply. Women who were hearty enough might bear ten children or more! Many women died young because they could not survive multiple pregnancies or the complications of childbirth.

In the homes of the wealthy, food was prepared by servants or slaves. The kitchen was located in a building apart from the main house to prevent fires and to keep the living quarters free of cooking odors and the tremendous heat created by the huge cooking fireplaces.

A woman who spun wool was called a spinster. Every woman learned to spin yarn as part of her education. If you were wealthy, your slaves did the spinning and weaving for the household. In this picture, a spinster threads a spool on a treadle-operated spinning wheel. The basket beside her holds wool that she has prepared by washing and carding (the wool was pulled through the steel bristles of the carder to remove tangles and dirt). By tapping a foot pedal, she moves the wheel and spins the yarn into thread.

The many menial tasks that kept the homes and city operating smoothly were performed by servants and slaves. They assisted in every facet of life, such as baking bread at the Raleigh Tavern, removing chamber pots at Wetherburn's Tavern, braiding baskets and shoeing horses, and raising their master's children.

SLAVES

In the 1770s, half of Williamsburg's population consisted of slaves. Henry Wetherburn relied on twelve slaves to manage his tavern. They cooked, served, cleaned, tended his garden, ran his dairy, and cared for customers' horses. Peyton Randolph owned twenty-seven slaves, nine of whom he probably hired out for work elsewhere in the city. Like other men of his class, Randolph designated one slave to be his manservant. This slave cared for Randolph completely, beginning by shaving him when he awoke, and finishing by stoking the coals in the fireplace when he went to bed. Slaves served as wet nurses and nursemaids. They often developed warm relationships with the children they raised for their masters.

Most of the slaves working in Williamsburg were bought at auctions held on Market Square. Their living conditions were crude and crowded. Their clothing was made of rough cloth spun by a slave trained in that craft.

Although their life was never as bleak as that of a plantation slave, Williamsburg slaves often worked fourteen-hour days, could be whipped at will by their masters, were not allowed to marry legally, and could be sold at any time. Even those slaves with kind masters who taught them to read, gave them responsibilities, and embraced them as part of the family were not free. They were considered property, not human beings. Although it happened rarely, slaves could be freed by their masters. At one time, six free blacks lived and worked in Williamsburg.

A popular Williamsburg entertainment during Publick Times was the theater (the first in colonial America). Plays were never serious; even the tragedies were farces that poked fun at society. They were interactive, the actors often stopping the action of the play to talk to the audience. The audience was encouraged to boo and hiss at appropriate moments, and often the actors would boo and hiss back. Between acts, magicians, jugglers, and trapeze artists provided more amusement for the audience.

PUBLICK TIMES

During Publick Times in the spring and the fall when the government convened, Williamsburg burst forth with life. Its population swelled to six thousand.

The halls of the capitol overflowed with people clamoring to see the court in session. The many taverns were crowded during the day with merchants, lawyers, and planters discussing pressing political and economic matters. During the evenings the tables were pushed back and serious conversation gave way to laughter and dancing feet. A small group of musicians played as the Williamsburg elite danced minuets, quadrilles, and the Virginia Reel.

Duke of Gloucester Street became a hustle-bustle of activity: a woman emerging from a milliner's shop with a new hat or dress, a man adjusting his newly curled wig as he hurried down the steps of the barber and peruke maker, small groups of men discussing the political situation of the day, slaves carrying supplies they had purchased at shops and markets for their masters' dinners.

GOVERNING VIRGINIA

The government in Williamsburg had to oversee the huge territory that stretched from the East Coast to the Mississippi River. The Virginia Colony included large plantations on the James River and small farms in the Shenandoah Valley. It included backwoods farmers, plantation owners, small businessmen, craftsmen, and slaves.

Monticello, the home Thomas Jefferson designed and built, was the centerpiece of his five-thousand-acre plantation.

THE VIRGINIA ARISTOCRACY GOVERNS

All regions were represented in the House of Burgesses, but the majority of burgesses were rich, conservative, landed gentry with large Tidewater plantations along the coast. The plantation was a training ground for leadership. Running a plantation was like running a small town. The plantation owner had to be farmer, businessman, diplomat, and psychologist. He knew from a young age that he had been born to a special position in society, with both rewards and responsibilities. It is no coincidence that many of the great men of the Revolution, such as George Washington,

Thomas Jefferson, James Mason, Peyton Randolph, and Richard Henry Lee, were Virginia plantation owners.

Because the English government was in a state of constant turmoil and civil war from the time Jamestown became the capital of Virginia in 1607, the American colonies were generally left alone to govern themselves. The burgesses operated with little English interference. As a result, the colonists came to expect that they had the right to make their own decisions.

MERCANTILISM

These ideas of independence were in direct conflict with England's plan for her colonies. This grand plan was called *mercantilism*. To become richer and more powerful, countries such as England conquered territories and set up colonies. The colonies were to supply silk, sugar, spices, gold, timber, tar, and rice to the mother country for very little money or for credit. English ships carried these raw materials to the mother country to be manufactured into goods, and then transported them back to be sold to the colonists at higher prices.

ACTS OF TRADE AND NAVIGATION

To make sure that the colonies traded only with England and not with other European countries, starting in 1651 Parliament passed a series of Navigation Acts. The colonies were required to sell their raw material to England only and to buy only English goods. They had to ship only on English ships to English ports. Duties were added to goods from other parts of Europe before they were shipped to the colonies, which made them so expensive that even the expensive English goods were cheaper by comparison. Parliament passed laws forbidding colonies to set up their own industries. It did not want colonial industries to compete with those of the mother country. (The southern colonies were not greatly affected by the manufacturing law because their economy was based on agriculture—the production of tobacco or rice.) All of these trade laws were enacted to protect England's commercial monopoly and to make sure her manufacturers, merchants, bankers, shipbuilders, and shippers made great profits. These laws were intended to enforce the colonies' dependence on England. The colonists saw this as an infringement on their rights. However, as it was difficult, if not impossible, for England to enforce these trade acts from across the ocean, the colonial assemblies only grumbled and looked the other way as many colonists (particularly in the North) smuggled goods and bribed customs officers to get around the laws.

Unlike other colonies, Virginia could not ignore the trade laws. Because tobacco cultivation proved so profitable in the early years, Virginia grew little else and developed no other industries. When the Navigation Acts cut off her European market, she was forced to sell only to England and accept England's low prices for tobacco and high prices for English goods. English merchants paid planters in English goods instead of paying in cash. The planters shipped tobacco to the English merchants, who used the proceeds of the sale to buy the wares the planters requested. Since the tobacco seldom brought in enough money to cover the list of goods that the planter ordered, and the merchant always supplied them anyway, the planter owed the merchant for the difference. Under this system, the planters fell deeper and deeper in debt. Thomas

Juſt Imported · from *LONDON*

And to be ſold by

JOHN GREENHOW, at his Store near the Church in *Williamſburg*
for ready money only,

VIZ.

WHITE Callico
   Iriſh Linnens
Blue Cotton
Red ditto
Stuffs of different Kinds for
  womens gowns
Cruels and Marking Canvas
Handkerchiefs, blue
Handkerchiefs, red
Blankets of all forts & fizes
Wool cloaks
Ready made ſhirts
Fine mens ſtockings, blue
Ditto, brown
Ditto, red
Ditto, white
Haberdaſhery
Single and double Bed Blankets
Faſhionable mens and boys hats
Low priced Hats
Fine Night Caps
Feathers for Ladies Hats
Blue feathers
White feathers
Oſtrich feathers
Lateſt faſhion aprons, plain
Ditto, check'd
A very complete aſſortment of caps,
  in the neweſt taſte
Steel Sciſſars
Sciſſar ſnuffers
Laces of all Kinds
Livery lace
Variety of figured ribands
Variety of plain ditto
Trimming for Ladies gowns
Shirt and Waiſt Coat Buttons
Gilt and ſeveral other ſorts of
  faſhionable Buttons
A very fancy aſſortment of
  paper boxes
Baſkets
Wool cards
Smoothing irons
Milliners common needles
Fine Needles and Pins
Needle caſes
Silver Thimbles
Superfine Hyſon, Darjeeling,
  and Oolong Teas
Genuine freſh drugs
Sugar, refined
Cinnamon, Cloves, and Nutmegs
Figs
Confectionary of all forts
Mixed ſweetmeats
Brown Sugar Candy
White Sugar Candy
Black Pepper, Ginger, Fennel
Almonds
Pontefract cakes
Fine Chocolate
Candied Almonds
Licorice

Raiſins of the ſun
All Sorts of Spiceries
A confiderable aſſortment of
  flower roots
    Mixed tulip roots
    Anemoni
    Fine large hyacinths
    Double polyanthus narciſſus
    Crocus, blue and yellow
Beſt London Calf Leather
Leather of all kinds
Pigtail and cut Tobacco
Plain combs of all Sorts
Horn combs
Plain fans
All forts of wedding fans
Mortars and Peſtles
Elegent ſnuff boxes
Houſe bells
Candleſticks
Braſs deſk furniture
Candles, dipped
Ditto, mould
Myrtle wax
Toys of various ſorts
Dice and Boxes
Undreſſed Dolls
Dreſſed Dolls
Babies of all prices
Variety of Queen's china for
  children, ſets complete
Whiſtles for Children
Inſtructions for the Tin Whiſtle
Blank Books unruled of all ſizes
Memorandum books
A variety of children's books
Various other books and ſtationary
Slates and pencils
Paper of all forts & ſizes
Fine Prints by Bowles
Fine Prints by Hogarth
Playing Cards
Ink-Powder
Pencils
Inkſtands
Dutch Quills
Sealing Wax
Seals of all kinds
Fiſhing hooks
Powder flaſks
Borax
Brooms
Moſt forts of nails
Pumice and rotten ſtone
Emery
Files of all forts and ſizes
Chizells
Pewter, all kinds
Hardware, large aſſortment
Tin ſheats
Wire
Pewter plates, diſhes, baſons,
  and ſpoons of hard and common
  metal

Small and large tin Funnels
Wooden handled knives
Empty caniſters
Woodenware
Hard metal plates and diſhes
Tinware
    Coffee-pots
    Lanthorns
    Mugs
    Tinder-boxes
Iron kettles
Iron backs and dogs
Poliſhing powders
Silverſmiths caſting Sand
Great variety of glaſs, tin
  and ſtoneware
Crates of earthenware
All forts of China Ware
Large, noble and rich Chineſe Bowls
Delft Wares of moſt forts
China tea cups and ſaucers
Stoneware ſauce boats
Mugs
Bowls of all ſizes
Coffee
Seeds
    Globe amaranth, viola tricolor,
      and dianthus
    caraway, dill, fennel,
      marjoram, baſil, ſavory
Spice boxes
Split peaſe
Oats
Coarſe ſalt in bags
Large Quantity of the beſt Flour
Few caſes of preſerv'd fruits
Rice
Pickling Jars of all Sorts
  for Family Uſe
Sponges
Glaſs Bottles
Bottle Corks
Waſh balls
Soap
Beſt painted floor cloths
Tools of almoſt every occupation
Garden tools
Wooden garden rakes
Bird bottles
Window glaſs of all ſizes
Hand Lanthorns
Looking glaſſes of all ſizes
All forts of caſt iron
Iron of all kinds
    Trivets
    Shutter dogs
    Hooks
    Pipe Kilns
    Skewer Racks and ſkewers
Coopers, Carpenters, Smiths
  and maſons Tools of all Kinds
Moſt forts of materials for
  tradeſmen and many hundred
  other uſeful articles

*John Greenhow published a list of goods he had just imported from
London. For easier reading be aware that the letter S looks like our letter F.*

35

Jefferson computed that at the beginning of the Revolution, Virginians were in debt to British merchants for over two million English pounds.

Even though England monopolized Virginia's trade, the British government proved to be distant, disinterested, and inefficient in other matters regarding her largest colony. As a result, by 1760, Virginians had ruled themselves for more than 150 years. In Williamsburg, the burgesses determined taxes and paid the salary of the royal governor (which gave the colonists some control over him). In fact, the burgesses made all the laws affecting the colony of Virginia.

This autonomy was not destined to last forever. A conflict arose when England successfully fought to push France out of North America and wanted the American colonies to pay for it.

THE FINAL STRAW: PAYING FOR THE FRENCH AND INDIAN WAR

In 1748, France and England were the major powers left battling for control of the territories in North America. At that time, the French started building forts in Ohio to try to link their holdings in Canada, Illinois, and New Orleans. England feared the French influence in America. In a series of small wars around the world and finally in 1763 in the Seven Years' War (Americans call it the French and Indian War), England acquired all of France's territories east of the Mississippi.

By winning the war, England no longer had to worry about a French threat, but she did have to worry about hostile Indians who had allied themselves with the French and whose lands were being taken by the settlers. The solution—stationing ten thousand British troops to protect the settlers on the newly acquired lands—was expensive. Who should pay for these troops? Who should help pay for the French and Indian War? Who should help pay for the growing English navy? England's answer to these questions was: the colonists.

The colonists did not want to pay. They doubted that the war was fought for them. They didn't need British troops for protection. The French and Indian War showed them that they could defend themselves. They did not have enough money in their treasuries to support British troops in America. And besides, they wondered what good ten thousand troops would do across such an extensive border. Many colonists suspected that the British troops were being placed in America to control the colonists themselves!

THE STAMP ACT:
TAXATION WITHOUT REPRESENTATION

Parliament decided that the best way to raise money to pay the British war debt and manage the new territory would be to tax the colonists on all colonial newspapers, pamphlets, licenses, and commercial and legal documents. This money-making scheme was called the Stamp Act because a large blue paper seal or stamp was affixed to the papers when the tax was paid.

The dreaded stamp

Printer

Colonial printers played an influential part in stirring up the Revolution. They printed pamphlets expressing revolutionary ideas and discussions of the colonists' rights. Williamsburg's printers published political pamphlets such as Richard Bland's *An Inquiry into the Rights of the British Colonies* (1766) and Thomas Jefferson's *A Summary View of the Rights of British America* (1774) which influenced public opinion up and down the East Coast.

They printed newspapers that informed readers how the British were treating (or mistreating) the other colonies. For example, they alerted northern colonists when the Virginia Colony refused to buy (boycotted) English goods in 1769. They informed the South when English soldiers killed five colonials in the Boston Massacre of 1770.

Left: The typesetter chooses letters from partitioned trays called cases. The letters are arranged according to how often they are used. The upper case *holds capital letters. The* lower case *holds small letters. The typesetter sets the metal type in a composing stick to form the text of the newspaper. The letters are backward and upside down. Setting the type for one page of the* Virginia Gazette *took about one hour. Pages of the newspaper hang overhead to dry.*

Above: To prepare the press for printing, the "beater" transfers ink from two leather balls to the surface of the type. He is called a beater because he "beats" the balls together to spread the sticky ink evenly.

It is here that Parliament made two fatal mistakes. First, it did not ask the colonists. Second, by passing the Stamp Act in 1765, it taxed the most powerful, influential, and outspoken men in the thirteen colonies. The act taxed powerful merchants for every bill of lading. This duty raised costs for every item they imported. The tax on newspapers inflamed the printers, who were among the most active revolutionaries in all of the colonies.

The reaction in the colonies was explosive. The colonists were indignant. England was planning to tax the colonists to pay for England's war debt and the colonists were not even consulted. But then, the colonists had never had a say in any decision that affected their relationship with England because there were no colonial representatives in Parliament. It is ironic that the same Parliament that had recently (1689) fought the king and won the right for Englishmen to be taxed only *with* the consent of Parliament was willing to impose taxes on the colonists *without* the colonists' approval.

The Stamp Act affected every person in Williamsburg. Even the more conservative leaders of the House of Burgesses, the plantation owners from Tidewater Virginia, were upset. They had close ties with England. They sold their tobacco to England and bought all their goods from England. They built their homes according to current English styles and wore the latest British fashions. Some sent their sons to England to be educated. But, even though they felt English to the core, they resented being taxed without their consent. They also resented England's economic control over them. However, as law-abiding citizens, most felt they must obey the Stamp Act.

Not every member of the House of Burgesses felt quite this loyal. Although in the year 1765 most Virginians felt very English, their ties to England were often weak. Many had lived in America for generations. Their fathers and their fathers' fathers' fathers had been born in America. Many colonists had come to America to escape from England—some from religious persecution, some from poverty. Many had gone out on their own into the wilderness and survived. Patrick Henry represented those Americans from the backwoods who had carved out lives for themselves. They were not going to pay a tax unless it was a tax they chose.

The Stamp Act set Williamsburg ablaze with impassioned discussions about individual rights and the power of the king. Because Williamsburg was the most important city in Virginia, this is where people came to discuss and resolve these important issues. Men such as Thomas Jefferson and George Mason had been debating the concepts of freedom and responsibility for years. As early as 1760, Richard Bland wrote that "under an English government all Men are born free, are subject only to Laws made with their own Consent, and cannot be deprived of the Benefit of these Laws without a Transgression of them."

These ideas would soon be expressed in George Mason's Declaration of Rights for Virginia and Thomas Jefferson's Declaration of Independence. Ideas that were to be the foundation of the Constitution of the United States were developed and debated in the libraries of George Wythe and other Williamsburg scholars, in the halls of the College of William and Mary, and in the Apollo Room of the Raleigh Tavern. The official debates, of course, took place in the capitol. The House of Burgesses represented the colonists; the governor and the Governor's Council represented the king and Parliament of England.

The Governor's Palace was built to impress the colonists with the prestige and power of their mother country. Dazzling in gold above the door, the royal coat of arms proclaimed British authority.

The Governor's Palace

The deputy of the king and the most powerful person in the Virginia colony was the royal governor. As chief magistrate of the

colony he possessed complete control over the legislature and could veto any of its actions or even dissolve it when he felt a decision threatened the power of the Crown. Nine royal governors reigned over Williamsburg from 1698, when it became the capital, until the eve of the revolutionary war.

Many of the early royal governors were highly educated, creative men. Francis Nicholson (1698–1705) planned the city of Williamsburg. Alexander Spotswood (1710–1722) designed the powder magazine, the capitol, and the Bruton Parish Church. Spotswood made peace with the Indians. He attempted (and failed) to reform land laws which allowed land speculators to buy large tracts of land cheaply and then divide them into small plots and sell them at great profit. Francis Farquier (1758–1768) was a scholar, musician, and humanitarian, who was popular with the people. His liberal ideas greatly influenced young Thomas Jefferson, who spent many evenings at the Governor's Palace playing fiddle with the governor or discussing new ideas. Governor Botetourt, Norborne Berkeley Baron de Botetourt, (1768–1770), began a much needed redecoration of the Governor's Palace.

Despite their opposing goals (they had the interests of the Crown to satisfy, not the interests of the colonists), most of the royal governors were greatly beloved by the people. Even during the years just before the Revolution, when tension between the colonists and the Crown was growing, Governors Farquier and Botetourt were often sympathetic to the colonists' protests. However, whether in agreement with the burgesses or not, when the burgesses defied England, the governors dissolved (suspended until a later time) the House of Burgesses. The revolutionary leaders seemed to accept the governor's anticolonial actions as part of his duty. For example, the evening after

Governor Spotswood had the entrance hall of the Palace decorated with a magnificent (and intimidating) display of 610 swords, guns, and pistols. The wealth and power of a gentleman of these times were often displayed by the quality of his weapons.

Governor Botetourt dissolved the House of Burgesses for protesting English tyranny toward Massachusetts, some of these same burgesses attended a birthday ball for the queen at the Palace.

The governors lived lavishly in the Governor's Palace. The imposing brick building was nicknamed the Palace by colonists who resented paying tax dollars to house British governors in such luxury.

The clerk of the Governor's Council would bring citizens' petitions (such as a 1769 petition to keep customs houses from being moved from Williamsburg to another site) to the governor's attention.

A stone wall completely surrounds the mansion, its outbuildings, and its gardens. Cannons flank the Palace gate. A doorman guards the entrance.

The colonists were very aware that no expense had been spared in decorating the Palace. The chairs were covered with red damask plaid—the latest in London fashion. The staircase leading to the second floor was ornately carved and the walls in the upper receiving room were covered with tooled and gilded leather. Large paintings of English royalty dressed in furs and silks adorned the walls. Although the Williamsburg elite were often friends of the governors, ordinary colonial citizens were not welcome in the Palace.

PALACE ENTERTAINMENT

The royal governors entertained lavishly and often. In fact, it became necessary to add a ballroom and supper room at the rear of the Palace in 1751. Governor Botetourt boasted to a friend that "Fifty-two dined with me yesterday, and I expect at least that number today." His cellars were well supplied with 3,200 gallons of wines, beers, and liquors.

Dinner at the Palace was a very special affair. An invitation might indicate that you had arrived socially or that you were of some political use to the governor. Women and men dressed in their finest clothes, including white wigs specially curled for the occasion. Dinner was served in the supper room.

A ball at the Palace was a gala event. A master of ceremonies introduced the two hundred guests as they entered. Musicians played on harpsichord, fortepiano, and strings. Men and women lined up on either side of the ballroom to dance the latest gigue or minuet. Dancing was an important skill in colonial times. It was a way of showing off.

The dessert table is beautifully decorated with marzipan fruit, cookies, and cakes. Guests "dessert" the dining room after the main meal; women retire upstairs for a rest, men to the game or smoking rooms for conversation, cards, and a smoke.

The butler to the governor was in charge of the household staff (twenty-five servants and slaves) and the governor's wine, spirits, food, and silver. He kept the household accounts and supervised the meals. Governor Botetourt considered his butler, William Marshman, so indispensable that he paid him the highest salary of anyone of his staff. When Botetourt died, he left Marshman his complete wardrobe (including fifty-six ruffled shirts and thirty-six pairs of shoes).

HOW DO WE KNOW?

The Governor's Palace pictured earlier is not the original building. It burned down in 1781. Architects and historians recreated the original building by means of a measured drawing of the Palace floor plan by Thomas Jefferson; a copper engraving (the Bodleian Plate) of the Palace facade, outbuildings, and gardens; the inventory of Governor Botetourt's furniture and belongings; and records of Governor Botetourt's butler.

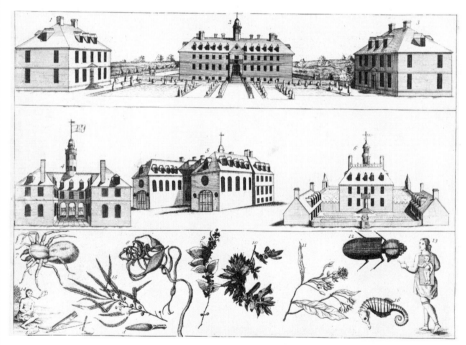

This print from the Bodleian Plate—an engraved copperplate made about 1740 which was discovered years later in the Bodleian Library, Oxford University, Oxford, England—gives historians a good idea what the original Palace and capitol looked like. Animals and plants of the region are depicted in the bottom row.

Governor Nicholson called the new statehouse the "Capitol" after the Temple of Jupiter Capitolinus in ancient Rome. It was the first statehouse in the new land to be called the capitol.

THE CAPITOL

The center of activity during Publick Times was the capitol. It was here that the General Assembly (the Governor's Council and House of Burgesses) met to make the laws that affected the Virginia colonists. It was here that the court meted out justice to citizens coming from all over the colony. Designed by one of the most creative royal governors, Governor Spotswood, the capitol was built in the shape of the letter H. The Governor's Council and General Court occupied one leg. The House of Burgesses occupied the other. A joint conference chamber was situated in the bridge that joined the two legs.

THE GOVERNOR'S COUNCIL

The chambers of the Governor's Council were elegant. The walls were paneled. The chairs were tall and finely carved. During Publick Times or during special sessions, the twelve council members took their places around a long oval table covered with an ornately fashioned carpet.

Luxurious? But, of course! The council members were chosen by the king to serve the Crown for their lifetimes. They all came from fine old Virginia families. They represented generations of conservative wealth and power. Their loyalties remained with England. Only three of the twelve council members sided with the colonists against England in the Revolution.

THE HOUSE OF BURGESSES

In the other wing, 126 representatives met in simpler surroundings in the House of Burgesses. The burgesses did not represent the king, after all; they represented the people.

This is not to say that the burgesses were common men. They were mainly aristocrats themselves. Many were landed gentry—plantation owners. The people (only white, male property owners could vote) elected them because of their superior education and leadership skills.

The burgesses felt equal to any English aristocrat. They assumed it was their natural right as Englishmen to govern themselves and, for almost 150 years, they did just that.

Patrick Henry in the Virginia House of Burgesses Delivering His
Celebrated Speech against the Stamp Act, *painted in 1851 by Peter
Rothermel. Compare the artist's vision to the photograph of the House of
Burgesses on the preceding page.*

In this austere chamber the greatest men in America's history rose from hard wooden benches to demand their rights as Englishmen. It was here that a fiery young orator named Patrick Henry stood to demand the colonists' right as Englishmen to decide for themselves which taxes, if any, they would pay, to demand their right to taxation only *with* representation. It was here that the birth of the American Revolution took place.

RESOLUTIONS THAT ROCKED THE WORLD

On May 30, 1765, a resolution was introduced in the House of Burgesses to debate the Stamp Act. The House of Burgesses had already been in session six days. Thinking that business was almost finished, some of the Tidewater conservatives, those who did not want to oppose British interference, returned to their plantations. This was the perfect moment! Patrick Henry jumped to his feet to offer his resolutions against the Stamp Act.

The house was electric with expectation. The young lawyer with the silver tongue spoke. "Resolved . . ." The first two resolutions demanded that the colonists be guaranteed all the rights and freedoms of Englishmen in England. The third and fourth resolutions demanded that the colonists have the same rights guaranteed to all Englishmen: that they be able to tax themselves, elect their own representatives to vote for these taxes, and protect themselves with their own police.

THE FIFTH RESOLUTION

The fifth resolution, which confirmed that only the Virginia assembly could impose taxes on the colony, was the strongest. Its passage would renounce the Stamp Act.

"Resolved that the General Assembly of Virginia possesses the only and sole exclusive right and power to lay taxes and any attempt to decree otherwise has a manifest tendency to destroy British as well as American Freedom."

Patrick Henry added these fiery words: "Caesar had his Brutus, Charles the First his Cromwell, and George the Third . . ." Here he was interrupted by Speaker of the House John Robinson's cries of "Treason, treason!" By linking George III with Caesar and Charles I, two leaders who were murdered for political reasons, Patrick Henry would have been speaking treason. However, a French traveler who was attending the session wrote that Patrick Henry never finished his sentence. He apologized to the speaker, saying that "if he had affronted the Speaker of the House, he was ready to ask pardon and he would shew his loyalty to his Majesty King G., the Third, at the Expense of the last drop of his blood." Henry continued that he had only his country's dying liberty at heart and, in a heat of passion, had said more than he had intended.

So convincing was Patrick Henry that the five resolutions passed—although the fifth resolution passed by only one vote. Peyton Randolph, the distinguished attorney general, was heard to remark, "By God, I would have given one hundred guineas for a single vote." If Peyton Randolph had had his way, that vote would have created a tie and Speaker Robinson, voting to break the tie, would have voted against the resolution. Randolph was one of many men who disliked the way England was treating the colonies, but who felt opposing the mother country was un-lawful. (He soon changed his mind and joined the revolutionary cause, becoming the first president of the Continental Congress.)

Patrick Henry was a clever politician. As soon as the fifth

A portrait of King George III decked out in royal splendor

resolution passed, he and his supporters reported the resolutions to newspapers throughout the colonies. He made certain that the colonies up and down the East Coast knew that the House of Burgesses in Virginia had spoken out against the Stamp Act.

The next morning, with Henry and most of the burgesses gone, the house met and the fifth resolution was stricken from the record. But it was too late. The news was out! Resolved by the House of Burgesses: Only Americans have the right to tax Americans.

This was the beginning. In Williamsburg, in this austere chamber, the colonists asserted their power and demanded their inalienable rights, rights that no one has a right to take away.

Patrick Henry's resolutions sounded an alarm for action. Virginia's defiance was an inspiration to the other colonies. The Massachusetts house invited all the colonies to send representatives to a congress to discuss the Stamp Act. For the first time, these men met as Americans—not as members of the Virginia Colony or the Massachusetts Colony. They met as Americans to demand their right to tax themselves.

THE STAMP ACT IS REPEALED

Throughout the colonies, angry mobs rioted at customs houses, preventing the sale of the dreaded blue stamps. Without stamped papers, no ships could leave America for England. Trade with England stopped. The English merchants were not happy.

In Williamsburg, the rage against the Stamp Act was

directed at Colonel George Mercer, who had come from England to distribute the hated stamps. An angry mob of merchants and county officials accosted a surprised Mercer in front of the coffeehouse now called Christiana Campbell's. As they rushed toward Mercer to seize and destroy the stamps, Governor Farquier came to his rescue. The beloved royal governor talked the mob into waiting a day for Mercer's response and proceeded to escort him through the agitated crowd to the Governor's Palace. Tension was high the next evening at the capitol. Mercer explained that he had been abroad and was unaware of the furor the Stamp Act had caused in the colonies. He assured the group that he would act only with the consent of the General Assembly, which meant he would not act at all. The Williamsburg merchants were satisfied for the moment. But very soon, they would have to show their muscle again.

The Stamp Act was finally repealed because the colonists had attacked the English where it hurt the most—in the pocketbook. When the colonists' actions against the customs houses stalled trade, the English merchants put so much pressure on Parliament that in March 1766, the Stamp Act was repealed.

The colonists were ecstatic. Several cities even erected statues of King George III. They were so busy rejoicing, they took little notice that Parliament had passed another act: the Declaratory Act of 1766. The Declaratory Act restricted colonial freedom even more. It gave the king and Parliament power to "make laws and statutes of sufficient force and validity to bind the colonies in all cases whatsoever." The victory over the Stamp Act was short-lived indeed.

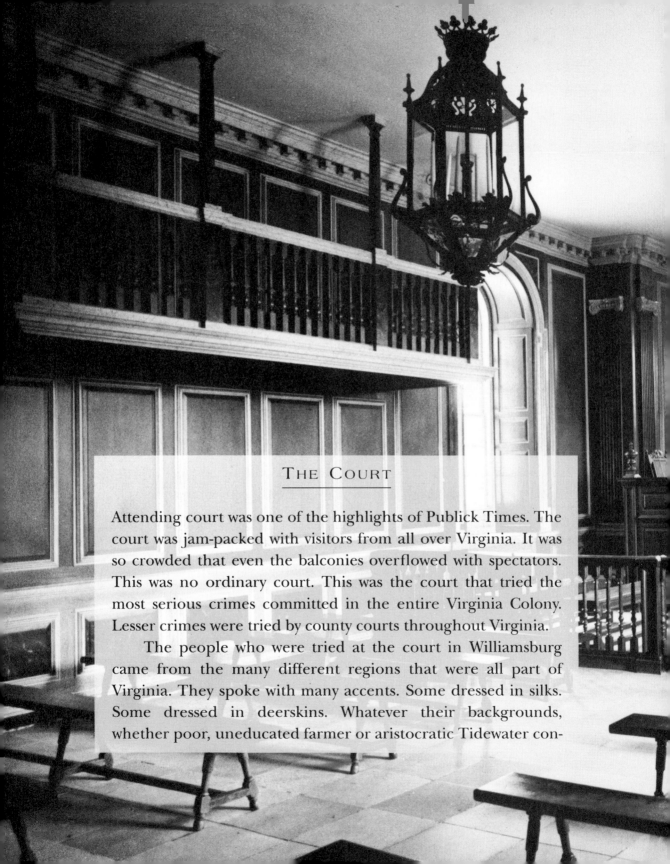

THE COURT

Attending court was one of the highlights of Publick Times. The court was jam-packed with visitors from all over Virginia. It was so crowded that even the balconies overflowed with spectators. This was no ordinary court. This was the court that tried the most serious crimes committed in the entire Virginia Colony. Lesser crimes were tried by county courts throughout Virginia.

The people who were tried at the court in Williamsburg came from the many different regions that were all part of Virginia. They spoke with many accents. Some dressed in silks. Some dressed in deerskins. Whatever their backgrounds, whether poor, uneducated farmer or aristocratic Tidewater con-

servative, they were entitled to a lawyer.* Their cases were tried by the governor or his appointee as chief justice of the court and the twelve members of the council who served as the justices. The accused learned his fate by watching the chief justice. If the chief justice put on a cap, the sentence was death by hanging.

Punishments were severe in colonial times. For stealing a silver spoon you could be hanged. Murder, arson, treason, piracy, burglary, forgery, and horse stealing were also punished by hanging. Criminals did not serve a sentence in jail (public gaol) as they do in modern times. They were either hung, banished to the frontier, or branded with a hot iron. Minor offenses such as gossiping, drunkenness, or not attending church were punished by imprisonment in the stocks and pillory. The public gaol (pronounced like our jail) was used mainly as a detention station for prisoners awaiting trial.

BLACKBEARD THE PIRATE

The most sensational case tried in this court was the trial of the fourteen henchmen of Edmund Teach, better known as Blackbeard the Pirate. In 1718, Governor Spotswood sent a navy expedition to capture pirates who had been plundering ships off the Virginia coast. A furious battle took place and Blackbeard was killed. His head was brought to shore swinging on the bowsprit of the British ship. One of Blackbeard's crew escaped, but the other thirteen were tried, found guilty in the court in Williamsburg, and later hung.

*Although they were allowed a lawyer, many of the accused represented themselves (often poorly). They reasoned that only someone guilty would need to hire a lawyer.

Minor offenses were punished by the discomfort and embarrassment of being on display in the stocks and pillory in front of the public gaol.

THE PUBLIC GAOL

The only long-term occupants of the public gaol were debtors. They were held for a three-week term. The gaol also served as a madhouse, and during the revolutionary war, as a military prison. For the times, the Williamsburg Gaol was quite humane. Prisoners were released from their leg irons and chains and allowed to walk about the prison courtyard during the day. If they had money, prisoners could even order food and drink from a local tavern.

The permanent occupants of the public gaol were the gaoler and his family. They lived in the front rooms and slept upstairs. Sometimes female prisoners or mentally ill patients also slept upstairs. The gaoler's pay was so little, he had to add to his income with other jobs. In 1771, the gaoler was also the organist at the Bruton Parish Church.

Prisoners might have slept on a bed made of foul-smelling straw in this unheated cell. Williamsburg winters could be brutally cold. Once a day a meal of cornmeal mush and salt pork was passed through a slot in the wall.

The English Bill of Rights (1689) gave Englishmen the right to a speedy trial by a jury of their peers (people from their own community) in an English court. The colonists believed they were guaranteed this same right but by a jury of their colonial peers in a colonial court. They soon learned that this was not a right they could take for granted.

In 1767, after the Stamp Act was repealed, Parliament imposed another set of taxes called the Townshend Acts. These duties on English paint, lead, paper, and tea were levied to collect revenue rather than regulate trade. The Townshend Acts allocated some of these taxes to pay the salaries of English officials rather than have their salaries paid by the colonial assemblies. Not only did the colonists see the Townshend Acts as more taxation without representation, they saw them as an attempt to limit colonial power over the royal governors and judges. Without the control of salaries, colonial assemblies had little control over English officials.

The colonists' reaction to the Townshend Acts was more subdued than it had been to the Stamp Act. The General Court of Massachusetts sent a letter to the other colonies urging them to unite for resistance. As punishment, Parliament dissolved the Massachusetts court. And then, in total violation of the colonists' rights, Parliament threatened to seize some popular colonial leaders and transport them to England for trial.

On May 16, 1769, the House of Burgesses supported Massachusetts by passing its own resolutions against the Townshend Acts. The resolutions asserted that it was Virginia's legal right to impose taxes on its inhabitants "with the consent of council, and of his Majesty, the King of Great-Britain, or his Governor, for the time being." It also declared the right to petition the king for redress of grievances as well as the right to rally the support of other colonies to do the same. The resolutions included a protest of England's illegal practice of seizing and transporting colonists "to places beyond the sea" for trial. Copies of these resolutions were sent to the other colonies. Governor Botetourt retaliated by dissolving the House of Burgesses.

BOYCOTTING: A POLITICAL WEAPON

Undaunted, the burgesses left the capitol. They met at the home of Burgess Anthony Hay, where they elected Peyton Randolph moderator of their new body. Then they reconvened at the Raleigh Tavern. Here they endorsed a nonimportation agreement written by George Mason. Under this agreement, no goods that required a duty, no luxuries, and no slaves could be brought into Virginia. The boycott of goods from England spread throughout the colonies. Boycotting was again an effective way to encourage English merchants to put pressure on Parliament to repeal offensive taxes. In 1770, the Townshend duties were repealed, except those on tea.

Although many colonists were angered by Parliament's imperial behavior—taxing them without even allowing them one representative in Parliament, using writs of assistance (general search warrants) to search homes, shops, or ships for smuggled goods, threatening to ship colonists off to England to be tried by an English jury with no witnesses for their defense—many still felt an attachment to the mother country. In fact, one-third of the colonists remained loyal to England, one-third favored independence, and one-third were undecided.

After the Townshend Acts were repealed, life in Williamsburg appeared to have returned to normal. But not for long! In 1772, a court of inquiry held in Rhode Island "with a power to send persons to England to be tried for offenses committed in the colonies" woke up some burgesses.

To avoid a confrontation with conservative representatives who were hesitant to act against English laws, Thomas Jefferson, Patrick Henry, Richard Henry Lee, Francis Lightfoot Lee, and Dabney Carr met in the evening at the Raleigh Tavern in 1773 to consider a plan of action. Thomas Jefferson wrote in his journal, "We were all sensible that the most urgent of all measures was that of coming to an understanding with all the other colonies to consider the British claims as a common cause to all, & to produce an unity of action: and for this purpose that a Committee of Correspondence in each colony would be the best instrument for intercommunication."

MOVING TOWARD UNITY:
THE COMMITTEES OF CORRESPONDENCE

Dabney Carr presented this idea to the House of Burgesses. He proposed (and the resolution passed) that every colony create a centralized Committee of Correspondence and that deputies from each colony should then meet at some central place to decide the action of all. No longer would the colonies be working independently. This significant resolution was the first step toward uniting the colonies since the Stamp Act resolutions.

Soon, Committees of Correspondence were organized throughout the colonies. These committees were vital to the cause of the Revolution because they created a network to convey information to all the colonies. Today we are used to instant communication over telephones, faxes, televisions, or radios. In colonial days, communication was limited to letters carried on horseback or by ship. By exchanging letters, the Committees of Correspondence actively kept the colonies informed of events throughout America. They exposed the misdeeds of Parliament and the king to all the colonies. The committees kept the fires of discontent burning.

THE TEA ACT INSPIRES VIOLENCE

In 1772, Parliament added fuel to the fire. It passed the Tea Act, a measure intended to keep the British East India Company from failing. The Tea Act gave the British East India Company a monopoly on selling tea. This meant that American tea importers and merchants were excluded from the tea business. If England could give a monopoly to one company, what prevented her from doing it again for another business? Williamsburg merchants were worried. England could drive all American importers and merchants out of business. The colonists were roused to action. The Committees of Correspondence urged all colonies to act.

And act they did. In Annapolis, Maryland, colonists burned the *Peggy Stewart,* a ship that transported tea. In Charleston, South Carolina, tea was landed but set in warehouses to rot. In Philadelphia and New York, crowds of colonists prevented tea from being landed. In Boston, 150 men dressed as Indians, stole aboard the tea ships, and threw the tea into the harbor.

In retaliation for Boston's protest (now known as the Boston Tea Party), Parliament passed an act closing Boston's port to all commerce. The patriots in Virginia could not sit by while their sister colony was being strangled. On May 24, 1774, the House of

Burgesses declared June 1, the day the Boston harbor was closed, a day of fasting and prayer. To punish the burgesses for supporting Boston, the royal governor, Lord Dunmore, dissolved the assembly.

BRUTON PARISH CHURCH

Thomas Jefferson had proposed the day of prayer at Bruton Parish Church not only as a protest against England's immoral action, but as a way to gather support for the Revolution. Even as late as 1774, some of the colonial leaders were hesitant to

actively oppose England. It was Jefferson's idea to use the power of religion to bring people together. Perhaps by praying together, they would side together against the English.

RELIGIOUS FREEDOM: NOT A RIGHT

In 1774, the Bruton Parish Church was *the* church of Williamsburg. There was no separation of church and state. Everyone had to pay taxes to support the English or Anglican church. If you did not attend church at least once a month you could be fined or locked in the stocks and pillory. It wasn't until 1786 that the Virginia legislature passed Jefferson's Statute for Religious Freedom, for which he had been fighting for nine years. The bill guaranteed that "no man shall be compelled to frequent or support any religious worship, place or ministry whatsoever, nor shall be enforced, restrained, molested, or burthened in his body or goods, or shall otherwise suffer, on account of his religious opinions or belief; but that all men shall be free to profess, and by argument to maintain, their opinions in matters of religion, and that the same shall in no wise diminish, enlarge or affect their civil capacities." Jefferson's Statute for Religious Freedom paved the way for the guarantee of religious freedom in the First Amendment of the Bill of Rights of the Constitution of the United States.

THE BIRTH OF THE CONTINENTAL CONGRESS

A day after the governor dissolved the House of Burgesses, the members reconvened in the Apollo Room of the Raleigh Tavern. During this historic meeting, the eighty-nine burgesses agreed that the abridgment of Boston's rights was an assault on the rights of all the colonies. They recommended that since their interests

The Apollo Room of the Raleigh Tavern looks empty and still today, but during prerevolutionary times, this room was alive with discussion and debate. It often served as the House of Burgesses in exile.

were the same, representatives from all the colonies should meet as one body to discuss the interests of all. They immediately took action on this idea and proposed to the Committees of Correspondence throughout the colonies that they appoint or elect delegates to attend a Continental Congress.

The Continental Congress met in Philadelphia on September 5, 1774. The Virginia delegation played an important part in the proceedings. Peyton Randolph, speaker of the Virginia House of Burgesses, was elected as the president of the Continental Congress. Patrick Henry made a persuasive speech calling for each delegate to abandon his colony's self-interest and work in the interest of all the colonies as a whole: "The distinctions between Virginians, Pennsylvanians, New Yorkers, and New Englanders are no more. I am not a Virginian, but an American," he declared. The colonies had come together as one.

"Give Me Liberty or Give Me Death!"

By March of 1775, it was clear that war with England was inevitable. At a convention of Virginia delegates convened in Richmond, Virginia, Patrick Henry introduced a bill for assembling and training militia. He melted any resistance with these stirring words: "Is life so dear, or peace so sweet, as to be purchased with the price of chains and slavery? Forbid it, Almighty God! I know not what course others may take, but as for me, give me liberty or give me death!"

Conflicts Increase

In the North, relations between the colonists and the British were turning violent. On the nineteenth of April, 1775, British troops marched on Lexington, Massachusetts, to arrest John Hancock and Sam Adams, two patriots the British considered traitors. Hancock and Adams were spirited away to safety while about sixty Lexington militiamen came out to defend the village green. Realizing they were no match for six or seven hundred Redcoats (British soldiers), they started to disband. In the confusion that followed, the Redcoats opened fire on the militia and killed eight Americans. They then marched to Concord to seize the weapons they knew the Americans had been stockpiling.

This time the Americans were ready. Strengthened by local militia, the Americans gave the British a tough fight. By the end of the battle, 273 British had been killed or wounded, more than twice the number of Americans slain or injured.

It is no coincidence that a day after the Battle of Lexington, on April 20, 1775, the royal governor of Virginia, John Murray, earl of Dunmore, took steps to remove the gunpowder from the Williamsburg magazine.

THE MAGAZINE

The magazine, designed in a pleasing octagonal shape by Governor Alexander Spotswood, was used to store pistols, muskets, gunpowder, and shot for the Virginia militia. During the French and Indian War, sixty thousand pounds of gunpowder and crated guns were stored here before they were sent to supply the militia fighting in the Ohio Valley.

Not only was Governor Dunmore aware of the violence occurring around Boston, he also understood what Patrick Henry's bill to train militia meant—war! In the middle of the night on April 20, 1775, Governor Dunmore ordered his troops to spirit the gunpowder stores out of the Williamsburg magazine and onto a British man-of-war in the York River. By removing the gunpowder, Dunmore was not only protecting himself against patriot fire, he was also destroying Virginia's means of defending herself against British attack.

A night watchman observed the troops and quickly alerted the city. Soon an angry mob gathered, ready to seize Dunmore and even kill him if he refused to return the powder. The crowd was quieted and sent home. But on May 3, Patrick Henry and 150 armed men marched on the Palace and demanded 330 pounds as payment for the gunpowder. Reluctantly, Dunmore paid the sum and then escaped to a waiting man-of-war in the York River. Williamsburg would see no more royal governors.

Not content to accept his loss of power, Dunmore sailed to Norfolk, the seaport of Virginia, and with the few loyalists and English seamen he had gathered, he made raids on Tidewater plantations. In November he issued a proclamation declaring martial law (rule by military authorities) and granting freedom to any slaves who would join him in rebellion against their patriot masters. Dunmore's proclamation only increased the colonists' hatred toward him. Virginians were terrified of a slave uprising. Knowing that Dunmore was gathering slaves, Indians, and loyalists together to make war on Virginia, the Virginians who had been lukewarm about breaking off with England were convinced that independence was the only course of action.

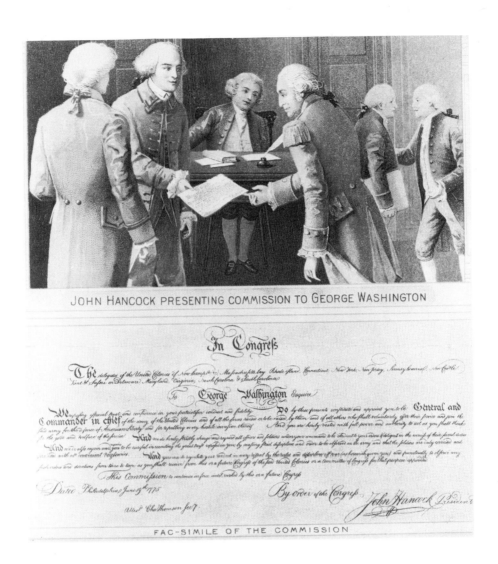

JOHN HANCOCK PRESENTING COMMISSION TO GEORGE WASHINGTON

FAC-SIMILE OF THE COMMISSION

WILLIAMSBURG LEADERS TAKE CHARGE

The Williamsburg gunpowder incident and the battles at Lexington and Concord showed colonists that the time for talking was over. If Americans wanted to defend themselves against the British forces, they needed to organize the ragtag militia in each colony into one national army. In June 1775, the Second Continental Congress chose George Washington, the delegate from Virginia, to be commander in chief of all the Continental troops. Washington was highly respected as a leader and a man of integrity. The Massachusetts delegates actively lobbied for Washington because they knew the strength of any military action as well as the success of the new colonial union relied on a strong alliance between the northern colony of Massachusetts and the southern colony of Virginia.

In Williamsburg, the House of Burgesses chose Patrick Henry as commander in chief of all the Virginia forces.

Virginia Declares Independence

Although there was little fighting in Virginia, during the following months, Bunker Hill (really Breed's Hill) and Dorchester Heights outside of Boston, the forts of Ticonderoga and Crown Point at the entrance to Canada, and Charleston, South Carolina, were the sites of intense fighting between the American militia and British troops. England's assaults on American cities and men showed Virginians that the American colonies had only one path to follow—independence!

On May 15, 1776, the fifth Virginia Convention met in Williamsburg and instructed their delegates to the Continental Congress to declare the colonies free and independent.

These Virginia Resolves stated that the colonies had tried to negotiate with England, but England had responded with "increased insult, oppression, and a vigorous attempt to effect our total destruction. . . ." And the Resolves continued: "In this state of extreme danger, we have no alternative left but an abject submission to the will of those overbearing tyrants or a total separation from the Crown and Government of Great Britain."

76

The Virginia Resolves helped sway the wavering delegates to the Continental Congress. Those who were still hoping for a reconciliation with England were convinced that there were no options left. They didn't want to live in slavery under English rule so they had to fight for freedom as an independent country.

DECLARING INDEPENDENCE

At the Continental Congress in Philadelphia, the Virginia delegate Richard Henry Lee moved, "That these United Colonies are, and of right ought to be, free and independent States; that they are absolved from all allegiance to the British Crown." The vote was unanimous. The final ties were broken. The Continental Congress chose Thomas Jefferson to write a Declaration of Independence.

INFLUENCE ON THOMAS JEFFERSON

While attending the College of William and Mary, Thomas Jefferson was greatly influenced by an extraordinary professor, Dr. William Small. Dr. Small introduced Jefferson to the writings of great mathematicians and astronomers such as Isaac Newton and philosophers such as Francis Bacon and John Locke. John Locke's ideas on government and freedom made a deep impression on Jefferson. In his *Two Treatises of Government* Locke asserted: "(1) People possess the natural rights of life, liberty, and property. (2) Government is created by the people and derives its authority from them. (3) The purpose of government is to protect the natural rights of the people. (4) When the government fails in its purposes the people may replace it with another—if necessary, by revolution."

Thomas Jefferson

DECLARATION OF INDEPENDENCE

Locke's influence can be seen on the ideas Thomas Jefferson so beautifully crafted into our Declaration of Independence:*

> We hold these truths to be self-evident, that all men are created equal; that they are endowed by their Creator with certain unalienable rights; that among these are life, liberty, and the pursuit of happiness. That to secure these rights, governments are instituted among men, deriving their just powers from the consent of the governed. . . .

*The Declaration that Jefferson wrote also drew heavily on Virginia's Declaration of Rights written by George Mason (approved by the Virginia Convention, June 12, 1776).

The beginning of Jefferson's original four-page draft of the Declaration of Independence

. . . that, whenever any form of government becomes destructive of these ends, it is the right of the people to alter or to abolish it, and to institute new government, laying its foundation on such principles, and organizing powers in such form, as to them shall seem most likely to effect their safety and happiness.

Clearly, forcefully, poetically, Thomas Jefferson explained why the colonies had to sever ties and become independent. These are the words that drew the colonies together to become the United States of America.

Clouds of musket smoke envelop soldiers during a reenactment of a revolutionary battle.

The war now began in earnest. The first shots had been fired in Boston, but the thoughts that shaped our Declaration of Independence and our Constitution, the ideas that became the words to influence men and inspire action, were nurtured and developed in Williamsburg. The great thinkers and leaders who began their careers in Williamsburg became the governors, presidents, congressmen, and generals who led our young nation to greatness.

PUBLIC GAOL

During the war with England, the Williamsburg Gaol was filled with captured British Redcoats, Tories (colonists supporting the English Crown), and accused spies and traitors. Henry Hamilton, English governor of the land north of the Ohio River and east of the Mississippi (the Northwest Territory), who led troops and Native American warriors against the colonists, was captured and brought to the Williamsburg Gaol in 1777. He earned his nickname, the "Hair-Buyer," by paying his Indian allies for American scalps.

WILLIAMSBURG LEAVES CENTER STAGE

For several years Williamsburg was the capital of the newly independent commonwealth of Virginia. Patrick Henry served as its first governor and Thomas Jefferson its second. When it became apparent that the city was too close to the sea to defend easily, a new site for the capital was chosen. In 1780, the government of Virginia packed up and moved to Richmond. After 150 years as the seat of Virginia's government, Williamsburg was suddenly reduced to a small, unimportant rural town. Even the war left the city untouched . . . until 1781.

In 1781, after ravaging eastern Virginia, the British general, Lord Cornwallis, marched into Williamsburg. He took over the house of the president of the College of William and Mary for his headquarters while he attacked the surrounding area. For ten horrible days, Cornwallis's soldiers looted houses and taverns and left the residents to starve. To add to their misery, a thick swarm of flies and an epidemic of smallpox wreaked havoc on the once vital city.

Several months later, Williamsburg became the center of military activity—this time under the command of General George Washington. The American soldiers and French forces that had joined them in the fight against England gathered in Williamsburg to prepare for their attack on the British at Yorktown.

THE TREATY OF PARIS RECOGNIZES U.S. INDEPENDENCE

When the sun dawned on September 28, 1781, the American and French forces marched to Yorktown. After three weeks of brutal combat, Cornwallis surrendered to Washington and the war was over. The Treaty of Paris formally recognized the independence of the United States.

What had begun as heated discussions in the Raleigh Tavern ended with a full-blown revolution and the creation of an independent country.

Fireworks celebrating independence shower light over the Williamsburg Courthouse.

Cities throughout the United States rejoiced. Williamsburg celebrated with a procession and ceremony. But with the capital moved to Richmond, Williamsburg was a shadow of its former self. No more fiery discussions on rights and revolutions. No more noisy taverns and crowded shops. No longer did the halls of the capitol echo with legal or judicial decisions. What had once been the heartbeat of the largest colony of the New World barely emitted a pulse. Williamsburg entered a period of decline.

Up from the Ashes

When the government left Williamsburg, many shop owners closed down their stores; many taverns shut their doors. Over the years homes and shops fell into disrepair. Buildings steeped in history—the Governor's Palace, the main building of the College of William and Mary, and the Raleigh Tavern—were consumed by fire. The former vigorous colonial town became a distant memory.

Fortunately, Williamsburg did not remain a memory forever. It took the vision of one man, William Goodwin, a minister of the Bruton Parish Church, to make Williamsburg whole again. In 1926, Goodwin urged the millionaire John D. Rockefeller to finance the restoration of Williamsburg, in order to "restore accurately and to preserve for all time the most significant portions of an historic and important city of America's colonial period."

This restoration began in 1926 and continues until the present time. Williamsburg looks just like the colonial town it once was—except, of course, the parts of life that were uncomfortable and inconvenient have been changed for the sake of the visitors.

The streets are now paved and have wide sidewalks and curbs. Every building uses electric lights and air-conditioning. Outhouses have been replaced with indoor plumbing.

But, you can overlook the modern conveniences and step back into the vibrant world of Williamsburg during the 1770s. You can feel the excitement in the air as you walk along the same streets as those extraordinary men who gathered together to lead the colony of Virginia and then all the colonies of America to independence.

$\mathscr{B}$IBLIOGRAPHY

Bliven, Bruce, Jr. *The American Revolution 1760–1783.* New York: Random House, 1958.

Bober, Natalie S. *Thomas Jefferson, Man on a Mountain.* New York: Atheneum, 1988.

Bridenbaugh, Carl. *Seat of Empire: The Political Role of Eighteenth-Century Williamsburg.* Williamsburg,Va.: Colonial Williamsburg Foundation, 1957.

———. *The Spirit of '76, The Growth of American Patriotism Before Independence.* New York: Oxford University Press, 1975.

Churchill, Winston. *A History of the English-Speaking Peoples: The Age of Revolution.* New York: Bantam Books, 1963.

Davis, Burke. *A Williamsburg Galaxy.* New York: Holt, Rinehart, and Winston, 1968.

Diderot, Denis. *A Diderot Pictorial Encyclopedia of Trades and Industry, Volumes 1 and 2.* New York: Dover Publications, 1959.

Earle, Alice Morse. *Home and Child Life in Colonial Days.* New York: Macmillan, 1969.

———. *Home Life in Colonial Days.* Stockbridge, Mass.: Berkshire Traveller Press, 1974.

Eaton, Jeanette. *Leader by Destiny.* New York: Harcourt, Brace & World, 1938.

Goodwin, Rutherfoord. *A Brief & True Report Concerning Williamsburg in Virginia.* Williamsburg, Va.: Colonial Williamsburg Foundation, 1980.

Gordon, Irving L. *Reviewing World History.* New York: Amsco School Publications, 1959.

Loeper, John J. *Going to School in 1776.* New York: Atheneum, 1984.

Miers, Earl Schenck. *Rebel's Roost: The Story of Old Williamsburg.* Williamsburg, Va.: Colonial Williamsburg Foundation, 1956.

Miller, John C. *Origins of the American Revolution*. Boston: Little, Brown, 1943.

Morgan, Edmund S. *Virginians at Home: Family Life in the Eighteenth Century*. Williamsburg, Va.: Colonial Williamsburg Foundation, 1985.

Morison, Samuel Eliot, and Henry Steele Commager. *The Growth of the American Republic*. New York: Oxford University Press, 1950.

Morris, William, and Mary Morris. *The Morris Dictionary of Word and Phrase Origins*. New York: Harper and Row, 1988.

Olmert, Michael. *Official Guide to Colonial Williamsburg*. Williamsburg, Va.: Colonial Williamsburg Foundation, 1985.

Rouse, Parke. *Planters and Pioneers*. New York: Hastings House, 1968.

———. *Virginia, a Pictorial History*. New York: Charles Scribner's Sons, 1975.

Rubin, Louis Decimus. *Virginia: A History*. New York: W. W. Norton, 1977.

Smith, Page. *A New Age Now Begins: A People's History of the American Revolution, Volume One*. New York: McGraw-Hill, 1976.

Spruill, Julia Cherry. *Women's Life and Work in the Southern Colonies*. New York: W. W. Norton, 1972.

Tunis, Edwin. *Colonial Craftsmen and the Beginnings of American Industry*. New York: Thomas Y. Crowell, 1965.

Whiffen, Marcus. *The Public Buildings of Williamsburg*. Williamsburg, Va.: Colonial Williamsburg Foundation, 1958.

Williamsburg Craft Series, Colonial Williamsburg Foundation, Williamsburg, Va.

The Printer in Eighteenth Century Williamsburg, 1978.

The Wigmaker in Eighteenth Century Williamsburg, 1979.

The Apothecary in Eighteenth Century Williamsburg, 1982.

Wise, Felicity. *A Williamsburg Hornbook*. Harrisburg, Pa.: Stackpole Books, 1973.

INDEX

Italic entries indicate illustrations.